For Sage Reshi, our newest reader —C.F.

For my nephew Kyle —L.N.

Text copyright © 2017 by Candace Fleming
Jacket art and interior illustrations copyright © 2017 by Lori Nichols
All rights reserved. Published in the United States by Schwartz & Wade Books,
an imprint of Random House Children's Books, a division of Penguin Random House LLC, New York.
Schwartz & Wade Books and the colophon are trademarks of Penguin Random House LLC.
Visit us on the Web! randomhousekids.com
Educators and librarians, for a variety of teaching tools,
visit us at RHTeachersLibrarians.com
Library of Congress Cataloging-in-Publication Data
Fleming, Candace.
Go sleep in your own bed / Candace Fleming ; Lori Nichols. — First edition.
pages cm
Summary: When Pig plops into his sty at bedtime, he finds Cow sleeping there and must send her off to
her stall, setting off a chain reaction of animals being awakened to move to their own beds.
ISBN 978-0-375-86648-7 (hc) — ISBN 978-0-375-96648-4 (glb) — ISBN 978-0-375-98767-0 (ebk)
[1. Bedtime—Fiction. 2. Domestic animals—Fiction. 3. Farm life—Fiction.]
I. Nichols, Lori, illustrator. II. Title.
PZ7.F59936 Go 2017
[E]—dc23
2014010947
The text of this book is set in 24-point Graham.
The illustrations were rendered in acrylic ink using a dip pen and colorized digitally.
MANUFACTURED IN CHINA
10 9 8 7 6 5 4 3 2 1
First Edition

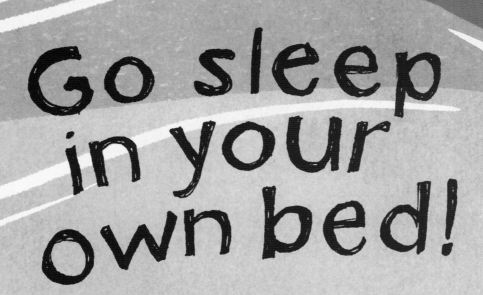

Go sleep in your own bed!

By Candace Fleming

Illustrated by Lori Nichols

schwartz & wade books · new york

Snuggled in.
Snuggled down.
Bedtime on the farm.

Pig toddled to his sty,
waddley-jog.

But when he
plopped down—
Moooo!
Who do you
think he found?

"Oh, hayseeds," lowed Cow.
And she tromped to her stall, *clompety-stomp.*

But when she snuggled down—
Bwaaaak!
Who do you think she found?

"Oh, fluff and feathers," clucked Hen.
And she straggled to her coop, *peckety-droop*.

But when she nestled down—
Naaaay!
Who do you think she found?

"Oh, w-w-w-h-o-o-o-a is me," whickered Horse.
And he shambled to his stable, *cloppety-plod*.

But when he settled down—
Mehhhhh!
Who do you think he found?

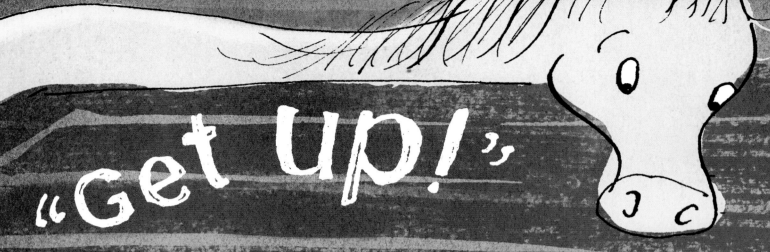

"Get up!"

whinnied Horse.

"Go sleep in your own bed!"

"Oh, baaah-ther!" bleated Sheep.
And she stumbled to her pen, *trippety-slump*.

But when she huddled down—
Arrrr-roooof!
Who do you think she found?

"Oh, bark and bellyache," whined Dog.
And he padded to his kennel, *sniffety-drag*.

But when he flopped down—
Meeeeooow!
Who do you think he found?

"Get up!"

woofed Dog.

"Go sleep in your own bed!"

"Oh, drat," mewed Cat.
And she tiptoed to her spot, *pittery-pat*.

But when she cuddled down—
"Here, kitty, kitty!"
Who do you think she found?

"Oh, there you are! Come sleep in my bed!"